ARTHUR'S
LOOSE TOOTH

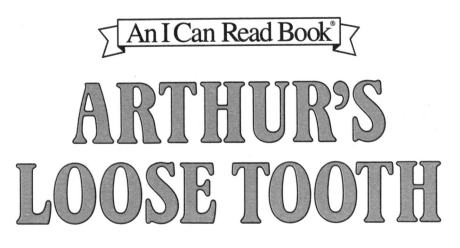

An I Can Read Book®

ARTHUR'S LOOSE TOOTH

Story and Pictures by

Lillian Hoban

HarperTrophy
A Division of HarperCollinsPublishers

HarperCollins®, ®, and I Can Read Book®
are trademarks of HarperCollins Publishers Inc.

Arthur's Loose Tooth
Copyright © 1985 by Lillian Hoban
For information address
HarperCollins Children's Books, a division of
HarperCollins Publishers, 10 East 53rd Street,
New York, N.Y. 10022.
Designed by Trish Parcell

Library of Congress Cataloging in Publication Data
Hoban, Lillian
Arthur's loose tooth.

(An I can read book)
Summary: Arthur the chimp is a little worried about
losing his loose tooth, until his sister and their
baby-sitter show him the real meaning of bravery.
1. Children's stories, American. [1. Teeth—Fiction.
2. Courage—Fiction. 3. Brothers and sisters—Fiction.
4. Babysitters—Fiction. 5. Chimpanzees—Fiction]
I. Title. II. Series.
PZ7.H635Aw 1985   [E]   85-42611
ISBN 0-06-022353-7
ISBN 0-06-022354-5 (lib. bdg.)
ISBN 0-06-444093-1 (pbk.)

To Katie Franklin

It was Saturday evening.

Mother and Father were at a party.

The baby-sitter was fixing supper.

Violet was playing
with her doctor kit.

She put a bandage on her doll's head.

"I am going to be a doctor
when I grow up," she said.

"What are you going to be, Arthur?"

"Vroom, vroom!" yelled Arthur.

He held up his arms

and made big muscles.

"I am going to be Captain Fearless,

the bravest chimp in the world.

I have THE POWER!" he shouted.

"Stop all that noise,"

said the baby-sitter.

"You are giving me a headache."

9

"My doll has a headache, too,"
said Violet.

"I think I will put him to bed."
Violet took her doll
and her doctor kit.
She started up the stairs.

Then she came back.

"Arthur," she said,

"will you come with me?

It is dark upstairs,

and I am scared."

11

"Only babies are scared
of the dark," said Arthur.
"Captain Fearless
isn't scared of anything.
Watch him use THE POWER!"
Arthur went zooming
around the room.

He bumped into tables and chairs.

He knocked over

Mother's sewing basket

and a pile of newspapers.

He knocked over

Father's pipe stand

and a bowl of fruit.

Then he tripped and fell.

"Arthur cut his lip,"

Violet called to the baby-sitter.

"He is bleeding."

14

Arthur sat up.

He put his finger on his lip.

There was blood

all over his finger.

"I'm dying! I'm dying!"

he cried.

"Quick, get me a Band-Aid!"

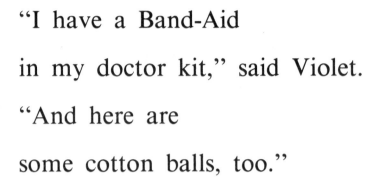

"I have a Band-Aid
in my doctor kit," said Violet.
"And here are
some cotton balls, too."

"Hurry, hurry!" yelled Arthur.

"My goodness," said the baby-sitter.

"You should not be scared

of a little blood!"

She wiped Arthur's lip

with a clean towel.

"There," she said.

"The blood is all gone.

It is just a little cut.

You don't even need a Band-Aid."

"I'm not scared of blood,"

said Violet.

"When I am a doctor,

I am going to cut people open

and fix their insides.

There will be lots of blood."

"I was not really scared,"
said Arthur. "I just thought
I had swallowed my loose front tooth.
Captain Fearless
isn't scared of anything.
He has THE POWER!"

"Hmm," said the baby-sitter.
"He should use THE POWER
to clean up the mess he made.
Then we will have supper."

21

"What is for supper?" asked Violet.

"Soup and sandwiches,"

said the baby-sitter.

"And a special treat for dessert."

"Only babies need special treats,"

said Arthur.

"Well, it is a good thing

you are not a baby,"

said the baby-sitter.

"Because this special treat

is bad for loose front teeth."

"I bet I know what it is,"

said Violet.

"What is it?" asked Arthur.

"You'll see," said the baby-sitter.

"Now clean up this mess."

Arthur started to clean up.

He picked up Father's pipe stand
and the pile of newspapers.

He picked up the bowl and the fruit.

He picked up Mother's sewing basket
and the pins and the needles
and the thread.

"Some of the thread got tangled,"
said Violet.
"Mother's favorite pinky-purple one
is all in knots.
Mother is not going to like that."

Arthur tried to take

the knots out of the thread.

The more he tried,

the more it tangled.

"I can get the knots out,"

said Violet.

"But first you have to come

upstairs with me.

I want to put my doll to bed,

and it is really dark up there now."

"Scaredy-cat!" said Arthur.

"Maybe I am scared of the dark,"
said Violet.

"But I am not scared
of a little blood."

"I am not scared either!"
yelled Arthur.

"Violet," called the baby-sitter,

"come help me make dessert."

"All right," said Violet.

She went into the kitchen.

Arthur pulled

at a knot in the thread.

The thread broke off.

He pulled at another knot.

More thread broke off.

After a while

there was broken thread

all over Arthur.

There was hardly any thread

on the spool.

"Maybe I *should*

let Violet do it," said Arthur.

He took the spool of thread
into the kitchen.
Violet was dipping apples
into a big pot.
"Guess what we are having
for dessert," said Violet.
"It is your favorite treat!
It is taffy apples!"
"Taffy apples!" said Arthur.
"I can't eat taffy apples
with a loose tooth!
It might get stuck in the taffy!"

32

"Well, if it gets stuck,
you can pull it out,"
said Violet.

"I don't want to pull it out,"
said Arthur.

"What are you looking at, anyway?"

"I am looking at the thread, Arthur,"
said Violet.
"There is hardly any left
on the spool.
Mother is not going to like that
one bit!"

"I know," said Arthur.

"Nothing is any good for me.

I couldn't get the knots out.

I can't eat the taffy apples.

All my luck has gone away."

"If your tooth came out,
you could eat the taffy apples,"
said the baby-sitter.
"Then the tooth fairy
would leave fifty cents
under your pillow.
You could buy some more thread."

Arthur wiggled his tooth.

"It's not ready to come out,"
he said.

"Let me see," said Violet.

Arthur wiggled his tooth some more.

"It looks ready," said Violet.

"It's very loose,"

said the baby-sitter.

"It's just about hanging in there."

39

"But if it comes out, there will be
lots of blood," said Arthur.

"I thought you said
you were not scared," said Violet.

"I'm not! I'm not!" yelled Arthur.

"I just don't like the way it looks."

"I know," said Violet.

"I don't like the way the dark looks.
It looks like creepy crawlies
waiting to get me.
But if I go into the dark
even if it scares me,
that means I am really brave."

"Who told you that?" asked Arthur.

"I did," said the baby-sitter.

"Anybody can do things
they are not afraid of.

But only brave people
do things they are scared to do."

"Well," said Arthur,

"I don't believe you.

I think you are mean.

You made taffy apples

and you know I cannot eat them.

It's no fair!"

"She is not mean," said Violet.

"She said if I am very brave,

I can make s'mores for you.

You can eat s'mores

even with a loose front tooth."

"What are s'mores?" asked Arthur.

"You'll see," said Violet.

"But first I have to get some sticks

so I can make them.

I am going out in the dark

all by myself.

I am scared, but I will do it anyway."

Violet put on her coat.

"Watch me be brave," she said.

Then she opened the door

and went out into the dark.

"Arthur," said the baby-sitter,

"you can be brave, too.

You can go upstairs and get washed."

"What!" said Arthur.

"I am not scared

to go upstairs in the dark!"

"I know," said the baby-sitter.

"But sometimes I think

you are scared

of a little soap and water."

Arthur went upstairs.

He put the spool of thread

on the sink.

He turned on the water.

Then he looked in the mirror

and wiggled his tooth.

48

It was very, very loose.

"I wonder what s'mores are,"

he said.

"I bet they are not as good

as taffy apples."

Arthur washed his face and hands.

Then he sat down on the edge
of the bathtub
and looked at the spool of thread.
"I wish the tooth fairy
would come," he said.
"I sure could use fifty cents."

The kitchen door slammed.

"Arthur," Violet called,

"I have the sticks

to make the s'mores.

Now I am brave.

The creepy crawlies

didn't even try to get me!"

Arthur thought about being brave.

He thought about the tooth fairy

and fifty cents under his pillow.

He wiggled his tooth with his fingers.

He wiggled it with his tongue.

Then he sighed and pulled

a long piece of pinky-purple thread

from the spool.

He wrapped one end

around the doorknob.

He tied the other end

around his loose tooth.

He closed his eyes and waited.

"Arthur," called the baby-sitter,
"come down for supper."
Arthur did not answer.

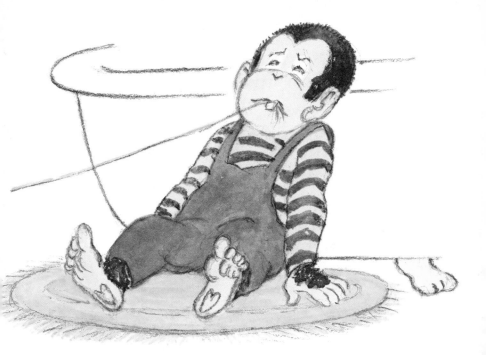

"Arthur," called the baby-sitter,

"come down right now."

Arthur still did not answer.

The baby-sitter came up the stairs.

She knocked at the bathroom door.

"Arthur, come out of there,"

she said.

Arthur kept his eyes tight shut.

He did not say a word.

"I'm coming in,"

said the baby-sitter.

She turned the knob

on the bathroom door.

The thread around the knob jerked.

It jerked so hard,

it yanked Arthur's tooth

right out of his mouth.

"It's out! It's out!"

shouted Arthur.

He held his tooth in his hand

and put his tongue

in the empty space.

"See?" he said to the baby-sitter.

"I told you I'm not afraid of blood!"

"Well then, Captain Fearless,"

said the baby-sitter,

"you can open your eyes and look

now that you really are brave."

Arthur opened his eyes.

There was a little blood on his hand,

and a little on his tooth.

It did not scare him one bit.

Arthur and the baby-sitter
went downstairs for supper.
"I pulled my tooth out,"
Arthur said to Violet.
"I was very brave."

"Yes, he was," said the baby-sitter.
"Now he can have s'mores
and taffy apples for dessert!"

After supper

the baby-sitter built a fire.

Violet showed Arthur

how to make s'mores.

"First you toast a marshmallow,"

said Violet.

"Next you put some chocolate

on a graham cracker.

Then you put the marshmallow

on the chocolate

and another graham cracker on top.

It tastes so good you want some more!

That's why they are called s'mores!"

So Violet, the baby-sitter,
and Arthur toasted marshmallows
and made s'mores.

Then they all sat around the fire
and ate the taffy apples
and the s'mores.
It was very cozy.